BETSY ROSS'S
STAR

Read all the books
in the Blast to the Past® series!

BLAST TO THE PAST ®

TO THE PAST #8

By STACIA DEUTSCH
and RHODY COHON

BETSY ROSS'S
STAR

Illustrated by GUY FRANCIS

Aladdin
New York   London   Toronto   Sydney   New Delhi

To my personal heroines:
Paula and Karen Deutsch.
With love, Stacia

One day I will fly away . . .
—Rhody

ALADDIN
An imprint of Simon & Schuster Children's Publishing Division
1230 Avenue of the Americas, New York, NY 10020
This Aladdin paperback edition June 2015
Text copyright © 2007 by Stacia Deutsch and Rhody Cohon
Interior illustrations copyright © 2007 by Guy Francis
Cover illustration copyright © 2015 by Fernando Juarez
All rights reserved, including the right of reproduction in whole or in part in any form.
ALADDIN is a trademark of Simon & Schuster, Inc., and related
logo is a registered trademark of Simon & Schuster, Inc.
BLAST TO THE PAST is a registered trademark of Stacia Deutsch and Rhody Cohon.
For information about special discounts for bulk purchases, please contact
Simon & Schuster Special Sales at 1-866-506-1949 or business@simonandschuster.com.
The Simon & Schuster Speakers Bureau can bring authors to your live event. For more
information or to book an event contact the Simon & Schuster Speakers Bureau
at 1-866-248-3049 or visit our website at www.simonspeakers.com.
Series design by Jeanine Henderson
The text of this book was set in Minion Pro.
Manufactured in the United States of America 0319 OFF
4 6 8 10 9 7 5 3
Library of Congress Control Number 2014952618
ISBN 978-1-4424-9541-8 (pbk)
ISBN 978-1-4424-9349-0 (eBook)

Contents

Time Travel

If you said to me, "Hey, Abigail! What's your favorite thing in the whole world?" I would have to answer, "History Club."

History Club is way better than art projects. Better than mini golf. Even better than eating pizza with sausage and extra cheese.

After school on Mondays, our third-grade teacher, Mr. Caruthers, sends three of my friends and me on a mission back in time. Jacob, his twin brother Zack, Bo, and I call our top secret time-travel adventures "History Club."

And our teacher, Mr. Caruthers, is so super cool, we call him "Mr. C."

One day a woman named Babs Magee stole a

time-travel computer that Mr. C invented in his laboratory under the school gym. Now she's popping around history, visiting important people on a list of names that Mr. C made.

Babs Magee wants to be famous. But she doesn't want to work for it. She'd rather steal other people's inventions or ideas.

It's a lame way to get famous.

When Mr. C discovered what Babs Magee was doing, he knew he needed to keep history straight. Since he is too busy working on a new invention, he asked Bo, Jacob, Zack, and me to help him out. It's our job to go back in time and convince those famous Americans not to give up their dreams.

Mr. C gave us a brand-new time-travel computer. It looks like a handheld video game with a larger screen and extra buttons. When we put a special cartridge in the back, a glowing green hole opens and we jump through time. Taking the cartridge out brings us home again.

We have two hours to get the task done. So far we've been really lucky. On all our adventures, Jacob,

Zack, Bo, and I have managed to keep history on track. We've foiled Babs Magee's schemes, and landed back at school with seconds to spare.

Today is Monday. I can hardly wait for school to end and History Club to begin.

①

Monday

Something funky was going on. Sure, to anyone else sitting in our third-grade social studies class, things seemed normal. But I could tell. They weren't normal at all.

Mr. C was sitting on the edge of his desk, like usual.

His hair was messy. His suit a disaster. His bow tie sideways. All normal.

He'd been five minutes late to class, just like he was every Monday.

So what was the problem? It was the question he asked to start the period.

It was more like a nonquestion. It was a statement, really. He said, "Share something you know about

Elizabeth Claypoole." At our blank stares, he cleared his throat and said, "You know her by the name Betsy Ross."

Most people wouldn't think there is anything wrong with a teacher telling his class to share. But anyone who knows Mr. C and is really curious, like me, would be immediately suspicious. Mr. Caruthers always, and I mean always, starts class on Monday with a "what-if" question. Like, "What if Betsy Ross quit and never sewed the first American flag?"

I love Mr. C's "what-if" questions. His questions are the best part of social studies. Today Mr. C didn't ask "what-if" anything. That's how I knew something freaky was going on.

I sit at a table with my three best friends, Jacob, Zack, and the new kid in school, Bo. Bo's real name is Roberto, but no one ever calls him that.

I leaned over toward Zack, who was sitting right next to me. "What's wrong with Mr. C?" I asked, nodding my head slightly toward our teacher.

"What are you talking about?" Zack whispered back. "What do you mean something's wrong?

What could be wrong? Are we in danger?"

I slapped myself on the forehead. I should have known better. Zack is a worrywart. He gets stressed out about everything. "What's the matter with Mr. C?" He was going on and on. "Is he sick? Hurt? Do you think I should get the principal?"

Oh, man.

The thing is, when Zack's not worrying, he's very funny. He tells jokes and acts silly. Even his clothes can make me laugh. Today he was wearing a T-shirt, inside out and backward, with a pair of jeans. I'm sure he got dressed in a hurry, and knowing Zack, he probably figured he'd simply pretend it was backward day instead of turning his shirt around.

"Abigail," Zack whispered back to me. His voice sounded shaky and nervous. "What makes you think Mr. C has a problem?"

I decided not to stress him out further. "It's just that . . ." I stalled. "Mr. C is so messy today."

Zack's face relaxed and he grinned. "It's Monday," he reminded me. "Mr. C is always messy on Mondays because we have History Club after school." Then Zack winked at me.

"Oh, yeah," I replied as if I was just remembering. "I almost forgot."

Of course, the truth was I could never forget it was Monday or that we have History Club on Mondays. Like I already told you, History Club is my favorite thing on earth. And even though I pretended not to remember, I knew exactly why Mr. C was five minutes late and messy today.

I knew because of all the kids in our social studies class, Jacob, Bo, Zack, and I were specially chosen as Mr. C's secret helpers.

On Mondays, Mr. C makes the time-travel cartridge for our History Club adventure. He never gives himself enough time to make the cartridge and get to class on time, too. There is also a huge explosion that screws up Mr. C's clothes and hair. It happens when he puts the lid on the cartridge. Even though we've asked, Mr. C won't tell us why he doesn't just make the cartridge on Sundays. He'd have plenty of time. And he'd definitely be neater.

I turned to Bo. Certainly he'd know why Mr. C hadn't asked us a "what-if" question. Bo knows everything about everything. He likes to read and remembers all the facts he's ever read. Today Bo was wearing baggy pants and a T-shirt that said READING IS TO THE MIND WHAT EXERCISE IS TO THE BODY. Underneath it said that the quote was by some guy named Joseph Addison.

Bo was sitting tall in his chair, listening to the other kids in class share what they knew about Betsy Ross.

Matthew Abrams raised his hand and said he'd once read that George Washington came to Betsy Ross's sewing shop in Philadelphia. Apparently George Washington hired her to make the flag for the new, independent American country.

Matthew hadn't even finished speaking when I swear I heard Bo mutter, "That's just a myth. Historians don't even know for sure if George Washington was in Philadelphia at the time." He said that so quietly, I wondered if I might have misunderstood his mumbling.

I took a long, careful look at Bo. He's usually quiet

and shy, but I'd never heard him mutter and mumble in class before.

Cindy Cho stopped biting her nails long enough to say she knew that Betsy Ross had created the American flag's stars and stripes design.

Right after she said it, I definitely heard Bo mutter, "That's not a fact. No one knows for sure if she designed it or not."

After each kid in class told Mr. C what they knew about Betsy Ross, Bo would mutter about how it "wasn't a fact" or "wasn't proven," or "was just another myth."

It was the weirdest day in social studies ever.

"Jacob," I whispered across the table, "have Mr. C and Bo both lost it?"

Jacob didn't answer. He was doodling something on a piece of white paper. I looked down. It was a picture of our time-travel computer. Jacob loves computers. He's president of the school computer club. When we go on adventures, he is always in charge of using the computer to send us back in time and to bring us home again.

I considered kicking him in the leg to get his attention, but Jacob was wearing new-looking blue pants and clean white tennies. I was wearing shorts with these awesome cowboy boots that used to belong to my teenage sister, CeCe. I decided not to dirty his clothes or shoes by kicking him with CeCe's old boots.

I was going to have to ask Mr. C what was going on. I raised my hand, but Mr. C had already moved on. Oddly, though, Bo hadn't stopped muttering "myth, myth, myth" under his breath.

I put one hand over my right ear to block out Bo's grumbling and kept my left hand raised high in the air. After a while my hand got tired. Unless Mr. C grew eyes on the back of his head, he wouldn't call on me. He was busy writing out a time line on the blackboard.

The time line said "Philadelphia" across the top, but didn't list any actual events. It looked like this:

June 1776   May 1777   May 25, 1780
March 1870   Month unknown, 1925

Figuring I'd ask about the "what-if" question later, I lowered my hand and studied the blackboard instead.

When he was finished writing, Mr. C turned around to face our class. "Who can tell me the main reason Betsy Ross is so famous?"

He called on Shanika Washington. She said, "Betsy Ross is famous because she sewed the first American flag." Just as Shanika finished saying the *g* in "flag," Bo's head exploded. No, not literally, but close.

"NOOOOO!" he cried out. In all the time I've known him, I've never heard Bo speak that loudly before. "IT'S A MYTH!" Bo roared. "There is NO proof that Betsy Ross ever sewed the first flag!"

(2)

Fact or Fiction

In a very stern voice, Mr. C told Bo to meet him in the classroom after school.

I nearly laughed. I mean, it was time-travel day, after all. Jacob, Zack, Bo, and I were all meeting Mr. C back in the classroom after school anyway. It wasn't as if Bo was being punished by meeting with Mr. C after school.

Or was he?

I felt a bit like Zack. I worried about it all day. Maybe Mr. C wouldn't let Bo time-travel with us. Or worse, maybe he'd kick Bo out of History Club altogether.

The day went on forever. When the last bell finally rang, I hurried to Mr. C's classroom to find out what was going to happen.

Jacob and Zack were already there.

Jacob was standing off to the side of the room, holding the computer, studying the buttons. Zack was in the corner stacking his and Jacob's backpacks. I tossed mine casually across the room and let him add it to the pile.

And Bo . . . poor Bo. He was sitting at our regular table while Mr. C peppered him with a thousand questions.

"What do you know about Betsy Ross?" Mr. C demanded.

"Nothing," Bo answered softly under his breath.

Mr. C squinted one eye. "Bo, you proved today that you can talk loudly when you want to. I repeat, what do you know about Betsy Ross?" Bo simply stared at his feet. Zack, Jacob, and I were standing near the door trying to blend in with the wall. It was really uncomfortable watching our friend get grilled.

"Really, Bo," our teacher insisted, "you must know something about Betsy Ross. You knew enough to tell the entire class that Betsy Ross's fame is based on a myth."

Bo shrugged. In a slightly louder voice he said, "A long time ago, I read the basics about Betsy Ross and the creation of the American flag. But after I learned that there weren't any historical facts to back up the story, I never read anything about her ever again."

I really wanted to interrupt. Maybe I could help. . . .

Jacob saw me take a small step forward. He leaned over and whispered, "You can't say anything, Abigail. This is between Mr. C and Bo." He was right. I couldn't be Bo's lawyer. Bo had to straighten this out for himself. I sighed and bit my tongue.

Mr. C told Bo to look up at him. Then he continued his questioning. "You don't know anything about her? Not about her life? Or her three husbands?"

"Nothing," Bo admitted, dropping his eyes back down to study the tabletop. "I know a lot about the Revolutionary War, though."

Mr. C nodded, saying, "I know."

Zack leaned over to Jacob and me and said super softly, "Is Mr. C going to keep Bo here all afternoon? If we don't time-travel soon, we'll run out of time." We all knew that the computer only gave us two hours to fix history. Our time to travel was ticking away.

"Mellow out," Jacob whispered back at his twin. "Since we have no clue where we are headed, we'll just have to wait. Plus, we aren't leaving without Bo."

The thought that Bo might not be allowed to time-travel gave me a bad feeling in the pit of my stomach. "Bo always helps so much," I said. "We really need him."

Mr. C shot us a look that clearly meant we needed to stop talking. He turned back to Bo. "What do you know about the American flag?"

"I can tell you the laws about flags today. For example, it says in the United States Flag Code section eight (i) that you shouldn't print images of the flag on paper plates, or napkins, or things that will be thrown away—true facts like that."

Mr. C seemed impressed with Bo's answer. And yet, he still looked puzzled. "You can recite the country's flag laws, which were passed by Congress in 1942, but you know nothing about how the actual flag was created?"

Bo's cheeks became redder than they were at the beginning of Mr. C's questions. "No," Bo muttered. "I don't know anything about how the flag was created. If it's a myth, I'm not interested."

"Fascinating," Mr. C remarked. "And being historically minded, Bo, did you try to find out where the flag design came from or who sewed it?"

At that Bo's head lifted again. "Sure I did," he told our teacher. "But I hit dead ends everywhere. No one knows for sure who made that first flag. And if the historians can't find anything, why should I waste my time? There are so many other things I'm interested in. I'd rather read a biography or the dictionary."

"You read the dictionary?!" Zack blurted out from where we stood, completely stunned.

Bo turned to us and smiled. "Only when I'm bored," he replied. "Okay, I'm lying. I read it every day," he admitted sheepishly.

Zack started laughing. We couldn't help it; Jacob and I began to laugh too.

The tension in the room had been broken and Mr. C couldn't help but laugh as well.

"All right," he said at last. "It's time for you kids to go."

"Home?" I asked, scared that if he wouldn't let Bo time-travel, none of us would go.

"Of course not." Mr. C looked shocked at my question. "The four of you have another mission today." He reached into his pocket and handed Jacob a small square cartridge. It had a picture of a woman sewing a flag.

I whispered to Jacob that he shouldn't show the picture to Bo. He might start yelling about how the story is a myth and then his head might explode . . . again.

"Bo's not in trouble?" I asked, feeling totally relieved.

"I didn't say that," Mr. C replied, turning to Bo. "In the future, if you have an issue with what we are learning in class, you need to talk to me calmly instead of shouting out."

Bo nodded, silently agreeing. Then he glanced over toward the cartridge in Jacob's hand. Jacob didn't move his hand away fast enough. Bo saw the small picture and groaned. "After all we've been discussing, why do we have to go see Betsy Ross?"

"Because Betsy Ross is the next name on my list of famous people," Mr. C said, pulling his little black notebook out of his jacket pocket. "You know what that means."

"It means that Betsy Ross was going to quit sewing . . . I mean creating . . . I mean . . ." I actually didn't know what I meant. Suddenly I understood why Mr. C had been acting so freaky in class earlier. He couldn't ask the class, "What if Betsy Ross quit and never sewed the American flag?" because no one knew if she had done it or not.

I was starting to see Bo's point of view. "Why *are* we going to see her?" I asked Mr. C.

"I know!" Zack answered, full of excitement. "Because no matter if it's a myth or not, Betsy Ross is famous for sewing the flag. And if she's next on Mr. C's list, that means Babs Magee is going to try to steal her place in American history and get famous for sewing the flag instead."

"So what?" Bo jumped into the conversation. "Abraham Lincoln once wrote, 'History is not history

unless it is the truth.' Most historians agree that Betsy Ross probably didn't really make the first American flag! If Betsy Ross didn't really do it, who cares if Babs Magee says she did it instead?"

"Hmm," Mr. C said thoughtfully as he pushed up his glasses again. "Betsy Ross is important because American history is full of founding fathers, and she is one of very few founding mothers and female role models."

I immediately recognized the way Mr. C's eyes were shifting back and forth. He was gearing up for a short but important lecture. "The story in our textbook is that George Washington came to Betsy Ross and asked her to make the flag. Supposedly the meeting took place in June of 1776, right before the Declaration of Independence was signed."

Mr. C motioned for Jacob, Zack, and me to sit at the table with Bo. Zack started to complain about our after-school-club time ticking away, but Mr. C wasn't going to be stopped. He was on a teaching roll. I sighed. Now we might never leave. Or if we did, we'd probably only have ten minutes to visit the past before we had to get home to dinner.

"The people needed a legend that was more than just business. Betsy Ross's story is exciting and interesting. And"—Mr. C paused to shove those glasses up one more time—"no matter what really happened, you kids are going to make certain that Babs Magee doesn't take the credit for it."

He gave a very serious look at Bo. "I mean it, Bo."

Bo raised his eyes to Mr. C's. It was the first time I'd ever seen him look our teacher directly in the face. "I swear we won't let Babs Magee take Betsy Ross's place in history."

I could tell Mr. C wasn't completely satisfied with that answer. He scanned each of us one by one. "No matter what you discover while you are back in time, you must leave history alone. It is widely accepted that Betsy Ross created the first American flag. You kids must make sure it stays that way."

Bo's forehead was wrinkled and he was rubbing his chin. It looked like he was about to say something more, but then he suddenly changed his mind.

"Okay, Mr. C," Zack chimed in. "We promise not to

change history. Can we get going now?" Zack was tapping his leg, totally anxious to get a move on.

Mr. C said, "It's all right, Zack. No need to worry. It's going to be an easy mission. You won't even need the full time today. I'm sending you to nearly a hundred years after the Revolutionary War. You are going to the Historical Society of Pennsylvania's meeting in 1870. At that gathering, Betsy Ross's grandson, William J. Canby, gave a speech retelling the story passed down to him by his grandmother."

"How cool that his grandmother was Betsy Ross!" I exclaimed.

Mr. C smiled. "William Canby's speech talked about Betsy Ross's famous meeting with George Washington and how she created the first flag." Mr. C looked directly at Bo. "Three years later, Canby's words were printed in *Harper's Monthly* magazine, and by the 1880s, the story of Betsy Ross and the flag was in school textbooks across America."

Mr. C asked Jacob to hand him the computer. "You'll only need to make one stop on this trip." He popped a button off the front and twisted a few wires underneath.

"In fact, it should be so easy that I am going to reset the computer's clock to give you just one hour and thirty minutes. I will never be able to give you more than two hours, but I certainly can give you less. It's just as well, since we've used up some of the after-school-club time already." Mr. C finished making changes to the computer and replaced the button.

"What?!" Zack exclaimed. "We can't do it in an hour and a half. We always use the whole two hours. To be honest, we usually cut it really close."

Mr. C just smiled and handed the computer back to Jacob. "For this adventure, I am certain you won't need the full amount of time." He pointed to a big open space near the side of his desk. "You'd better get going."

Jacob slipped the Betsy Ross cartridge into the back of the computer. The green glowing time-travel hole opened in the floor. Smoke slithered across the floor.

As we jumped into the hole, Zack looked nervous about how much time we had. Jacob looked happy to be using the time-travel computer. Bo looked doubtful about the whole mission. And me . . . well, I was simply curious to find out what would happen next.

3

Fixing History

We landed in a big wooden room. Wood floors. Wood tables. Wood chairs. There were lots of people standing around—mostly men, but I also spotted a few women in the crowd.

There was a buzz of excitement in the room. Everyone was greeting one another with handshakes and pats on the back.

"We don't fit in here," Jacob remarked, looking down at our modern clothes. The men and women in the room were dressed in fancy, old-fashioned clothing. The men were wearing suits with hats. The women wore dresses, also with hats.

"We should find Babs, figure out how to distract

her while William Canby gives his speech, and get out of here quickly," Zack suggested.

"Sounds like a plan," I remarked with a smile. Usually I was the one begging us to come up with a plan. I was happy Zack made one first.

Jacob looked down at the computer screen. "I can't believe how simple this all sounds. I bet we'll be back at school way before our time is up." He glanced around the room. "Babs should be here by now. Just look for her coat and hat."

Babs Magee, for as long as we'd been following her through time, always wore the same yellow coat and matching hat. Mr. C said it was because she likes yellow and her outfit attracts attention.

Bo was silently scanning the room. He'd been talking so loudly and expressing himself so much today, I was surprised to see him standing quietly. Being curious, I wondered what Bo was thinking. There was something in the way he was wrinkling his forehead and rubbing his chin that made me wonder if Bo was doing more than simply looking for Babs. Bo looked . . . well, he looked like he was making a plan of his own.

I didn't have time to ask.

"There," Jacob said suddenly, pointing toward the door. "I think that's William Canby."

A man entered the room. He was dressed very much like the others and tipped his hat to us as he passed by.

"How do you know?" I asked. "I've never seen a picture of Betsy Ross's grandson, have you?"

"Of course not," Jacob admitted. "But he's holding a pile of papers that looks like a speech. I figured that was a pretty big clue."

"He's got you there, Abigail." Zack laughed, obviously proud of his brother.

I laughed too. "Good work, Jacob!"

William Canby was headed toward the front of the room. We knew that we had to be on our toes. There was no way Babs was going to let him get to the podium and give his speech, not if she wanted to claim that she'd created the first American flag instead of Betsy Ross.

I decided the best thing to do was to stay close to Mr. Canby. We could be his bodyguards. Then, when Babs made her move, we'd be there to stop her.

"Maybe this time we can finally snag her time-travel computer," Zack suggested. "Then she'll be out of the fame-stealing business forever."

"Good idea," Jacob told his brother. "She won't go anywhere else and Betsy Ross will forever be known for making the flag," Jacob added. "I heard that the Besty Ross House is the third most famous landmark in Philadelphia. Only the Liberty Bell and Independence Hall get more visitors."

Bo snorted. "Betsy Ross shouldn't be famous for something no one can prove she did." He was doing that weird forehead-wrinkling, chin-rubbing combo thing again. Bo was definitely up to something. I distinctly heard him say, "The writer Aldous Huxley wrote, 'Facts don't cease to exist because they are ignored.'"

"What do you—" I started to ask Bo what he meant, but stopped because William Canby was already headed up the few small steps to the podium.

He was about to begin his speech. The men and women at the Historical Society of Pennsylvania meeting were moving to sit in the wood chairs at the wood tables.

We had to stick to Mr. Canby like gum. Babs was here somewhere. But where?

"Mr. President, and gentlemen of the Historical Society of Pennsylvania," William Canby began when everyone was seated. "A number of persons who, like yourselves, are impressed with the importance of preserving every item of history relating to the origin of our beautiful national standard . . ."

I knew that "national standard" meant flag and was about to tell Zack that, when suddenly the door to the meeting room flew open.

Yellow coat. Yellow hat. It was that crazy Babs Magee.

"Stop the meeting!" she demanded. "William Canby was only eleven years old when his grandmother died. He can't possibly know if her story is true or not."

William Canby was super mad. It looked like darts were shooting out of his eyes, pointed straight at

Babs Magee. He waved his speech. "Not only do I have historical evidence that my grandmother sewed the first American flag, but"—he rustled through his papers—"I also have three signed affidavits by witnesses who say the story is true. Margaret Donaldson Boggs signed one of these letters. She is the daughter of Betsy Ross's sister, Sarah. Margaret clearly recalls hearing the story many times about Betsy Ross and the 'first star-spangled banner.'"

"Letters written by your family don't count!" Babs screeched. "I don't care if they are signed."

"The letters confirm the facts, ma'am." William Canby held his speech high above his head. "In June 1776, George Washington visited my grandmother at her sewing shop and asked her to make a flag for America. A receipt dated May 1777 proves that Elizabeth Ross continued in the flag-making business by supplying standards for the American navy. And although Francis Hopkinson claimed to have designed the flag in 1780, by the story I will recount today, I am sure you will agree that the Hopkinson design was not chosen.

"Whether you know her as Betsy Ross, Elizabeth Ashburn, or by her name from her third marriage, Elizabeth Claypoole, the evidence will show that my grandmother created the first American flag."

William Canby looked down at his speech and read from the last page.

"As an example of industry, energy, and perseverance, and of humble reliance upon providence, through all the trials, which were not few, of her eventful life, the name of Elizabeth Claypoole is worthy of being placed on record for the benefit of those who should be similarly circumstanced."

At that, I heard Bo mutter under his breath, "No matter what he says, or what her name was, the story is still just a myth."

Babs couldn't possibly have heard Bo. It was really weird when she said almost the exact same thing to the assembled crowd. "No matter what William Canby says today, the story of Betsy Ross and the creation of the American flag is a myth."

A tall, mustached man in the back called out to Babs, "If Betsy Ross did not sew it, who did?"

Babs put her hands on her hips and smiled a wickedly curving smile. "I did."

"If the flag was made in 1776 and today is 1870, that would make you more than ninety-four years old." Zack laughed at Babs. "You look good for your age."

Babs ignored him. But when a woman in the first row asked her beauty secret, Babs replied with a grin, "I eat healthy food and exercise daily." She was totally lying. Babs didn't look a hundred years old because, well . . . she wasn't even close to being that old.

"Can you prove *you* made the flag?" the same man in the back of the room called out.

"Yes," Babs said proudly. "There is a safe hidden in the home of a man named Sam Wetherill. Inside that locked box is all the proof I need to show that I, Babs Magee, am the real creator of the American flag."

"Balderdash!" the man shouted, interrupting Babs. "I am the grandson of Samuel Wetherill. I have no such safe in my possession."

"If we wait for history to unfold naturally, the safe

won't be found until 1925," Babs admitted. "But I can take you there today. I will tell you the story of how I met George Washington in 1776. I will explain how he chose *me* to make the flag. And then"—she smiled broadly—"I will open Mr. Wetherill's safe and show you the historical proof you need to know my story is true."

"She's bluffing," Bo whispered to us. "She can't possibly have any real proof."

This time Babs heard Bo and said aside to the four of us, "I have finally done it. You kids can't stop me. You might as well go on back to school and read all about me in your textbooks."

Jacob was staring at Babs's coat pocket. I could tell he was checking to see if he could find her time-travel computer. Babs winked at him, saying, "I'm not dumb enough to have brought the time-travel computer with me. It is hidden somewhere else."

"We have to help William Canby," I cried to my friends. "He has to give his speech!"

I glanced frantically around the room. People had gotten up from their chairs. They were all beginning to argue wildly about the flag and who had created it. William Canby was desperately trying to get everyone to sit down again and listen to him. Babs kept insisting she had proof and William Canby had nothing but a bad memory.

It seemed like everyone in the room was shouting.

Zack's eyes grew wide. "We totally messed up this mission," he said. "We should have caught up with Babs before she came into the meeting room. Now our time is running out. How are we going to get rid of Babs and help William Canby get everyone's attention?"

My mind was racing about what we could do. "To put history back on track, we have to get Babs out of here," I said.

"How are we going to do that?" Zack sized her up. "She's too big to shove out the door. And I think people would notice if we hit her over the head with something heavy."

"We could open our own time-travel hole and take her back to school with us," Jacob suggested. We all thought about it for a second. It wasn't such a bad idea. Her time-travel computer would be stuck here in 1870. She'd be at school with us.

"Forget it," Zack said. "It's too crowded in the room to open the time-travel hole." He bit his lip. "There must be something else we can do. . . ."

"There is something," Bo said at last. He had that look on his face again. His forehead was wrinkled and he was rubbing his chin. I suddenly realized why that look was odd. It wasn't Bo's normal thinking face. Instead it appeared that he had been planning something sneaky all along.

Bo asked Jacob how much time was on the computer.

"One hour left," Jacob said after checking.

Bo's face broke into a huge smile. "I bet they can argue for at least an hour," he said, grabbing my hand and pulling me toward the meeting room door.

"Wait up!" Zack and Jacob called at the same time.

Bo pushed through the crowd, leading us outside the room. With a slam, he closed the meeting room door. There was a small desk in the entry-way. Bo pulled open the drawers, rifling through each one until he found what he was searching for.

When he returned to us, Bo held a small key. With a quick twist of the key, he locked the meeting hall room.

"That should do it," Bo announced, surveying his work and tucking the key into his pocket.

"What are you doing?!" Zack asked, looking at Bo as if he'd gone crazy. "You trapped them all in the meeting room."

Bo simply smiled and said, "Yep." Then he calmly asked Jacob to set the computer to take us to June 1776.

"Why 1776?" I asked Bo.

"Well," he replied, "remember the list of dates and places Mr. C wrote on the board?" I nodded. "William Canby just told us what each one stands for."

"He did?" Jacob asked. "I swear, Bo, you have the best memory."

Bo smiled. "June 1776 is the date Betsy Ross claims to have been visited by George Washington and asked to make the flag. There is a receipt for flags with Betsy's name on it dated May 1777. May 25, 1780, was when someone named Francis Hopkinson claimed to have designed the first American flag. And March 1870 is where we are now, the time when William Canby gets Betsy Ross's name in our history books."

I thought back to the dates on the board. "Wow, Bo!" I slapped him on the back. "Good work. But wasn't there one more? Nineteen twenty-something?"

"Nineteen twenty-five," Bo told us. "William Canby didn't say anything about 1925, but Babs did!"

Like a flash of lightning, it came back to me. "Babs said that some dude named Wetherill has a safe. In that safe is something that she can use to prove she made the flag. The safe won't be open till 1925, unless she can convince everyone at this meeting to go check it out today."

I went over to the doorknob and made sure it was locked. Even if Babs convinced them to follow her, no one was leaving the meeting room until we said they could!

"Jacob, set the computer," Bo cheered. "The plan is

to visit each of these dates, starting with Philadelphia in June 1776."

"I thought we already had a plan," Zack protested. "We were going to find Babs, distract her while William Canby gave his speech, and get out of here quickly."

"The plan has changed." Bo was grinning wildly. "We have a time-travel machine and an hour to spare. And I say we're going to find out who really made the flag and give them their proper place in history."

"What about Betsy Ross?" Zack asked, a look of total panic on his face. "Mr. C said we shouldn't change history."

"We aren't going to change history," Bo said happily. "We're going to fix it!"

④

Zack

Zack tried to grab the computer away from his brother. "Bo's gone nuts!"

"Don't let Zack get the computer." Jacob quickly passed me the computer, like a game of keep-away. "I think Bo's right. We have the perfect opportunity to find out what really happened in history and set the record straight for all time."

Zack was coming after me. I knew I'd need to think fast.

Zack has been in a lot of after-school clubs. He usually quits them all after a few days, but I knew he'd been in spy club and weight lifting. He still ran track and won the award for being the fastest kid in third grade. There was no doubt in my mind that Zack was sneaky, strong, and fast.

If Zack really wanted to snatch the computer away from me, he probably could.

But I was clever. Fighting wouldn't change anything. We needed to talk about this. And I was going to make sure we had the conversation.

I held the computer behind my back. Zack dodged left, trying to grab it. Then right. I ducked and weaved as best I could, staying away from his octopus arms.

"Back off, Zack!" I told him, shooting him a look that showed I was serious.

"Pass it back to me," Jacob insisted. "I'm clear for the handoff."

"I'll take it," Bo called out. "Give it to me!"

"No," I said calmly. "It's mine now." I sounded exactly like my mom whenever she takes something away from me.

Bo stepped in front of me and said softly, in his usual shy voice, "I'm sorry if I made a big decision without you. This idea has been brewing ever since today's social studies class."

Bo rubbed his chin and wrinkled his forehead again in that suspicious look I'd wondered about. "I thought, *What if we could discover who really created the first flag?* We could give that person his or her proper place in American history. All we have to do to fix history is to come back here and give the correct speech to the Historical Society. Just like what really happened, the speech will be printed in *Harper's Monthly* and then put in history textbooks for students everywhere."

"But I promised Mr. C." Zack's voice cracked as he spoke. He was really upset. "He said we shouldn't change history and I promised we wouldn't." I remembered that Bo only promised not to let Babs Magee take over. In truth, Zack was the only one who promised Mr. C we wouldn't change anything.

"You won't be breaking your promise. We're not changing anything," Bo insisted. "We're simply fixing something wrong. That's different."

"Besides," Jacob added, "it's not like Mr. C will ever even know. By the time he's born, the history books will tell a different story about the flag and whoever made it."

"Why are you agreeing with Bo?" I asked Jacob, totally curious about what he was thinking.

"Because, as far as I know, we are the only kids on earth with a time-travel machine," Jacob answered simply. "We can witness history. This is an amazing opportunity to find out what really happened." He looked at me. "Come on, Abigail. Give me back the computer. We are losing valuable time."

As Jacob said that, I heard voices coming from inside the meeting room. It sounded like Babs was in a shouting match with William Canby. Bo was right about one thing: They probably would keep arguing for the whole hour we were gone. No one at the Historical Society meeting would probably ever even notice the door was locked.

Zack looked at me with begging eyes. "Please, Abigail," he whined. "Let's just do what we're supposed to do. Let's figure out a way to help William Canby give his speech and go home."

I sighed. It was clear, for the first time of all our adventures, we weren't going to act like a team. Either I was going to have to agree with Zack and try to convince the others to give up their plan, or I was going to side with Jacob and Bo. Zack would be the odd man out.

My head began to hurt as I struggled to make my decision.

Should we fix history? Or leave it alone even if it was wrong?

Should Betsy Ross get a place in our textbooks for something she might not have done? Or should we try to find the person who actually created the American flag and give him or her the credit?

ARGHHH!

Bo was full of quotes today, from his shirt to the quotes he'd been muttering along the way. Now he used another one to convince me. "Mark M. Krug once wrote, 'The historian and the detective have much in common.' Come on, Abigail, be a detective!"

"All right," I told the boys after carefully thinking about my decision. "I think we should go back farther in time to find the person who really made the first American flag."

Zack groaned. "But, Abigail—"

I felt bad going against Zack. "Look," I said. "It seems to me that Bo and Jacob have a good point. We have the opportunity to make a big difference for someone who may have been totally forgotten by history."

"But what—," Zack began.

I cut him off, holding out one hand like a stop sign. "I know what you are going to say. 'But what about Betsy Ross?' Right?"

Zack nodded. He seemed so sad, like I'd turned against him—and Betsy, too.

"Someone has to give a speech today. The only thing we agree on is that none of us wants it to be Babs Magee," I told Zack. "There is always the chance that we'll find out Betsy Ross really did create the flag. If she did it, we'll come back and help William Canby."

"But if she didn't," Bo put in, "we're going to make a new speech." Bo looked over at me. "I think Abigail should do the talking."

"I'll do it," I said. "If we find out that someone else made the flag, I'll give the speech." I actually like talking in public. I think it's fun.

"Fine. Just peachy." Zack put his hands on his hips. "Go ahead and jump through time, but I'm staying here." He looked at the meeting room door. "If you guys won't help William Canby give his speech, I'll help him myself."

"Oh, come on, Zack," Jacob groaned. "We are a team, and on a team when someone disagrees, the majority rules. Don't be such a baby because you were outvoted."

"I'm not a baby," Zack countered. "Take it back." Zack stepped toward his brother. His fist was clenched.

"Twins!" I put myself between them. "We're wasting time! We'll never find out who really created the flag if we don't get out of here now." I was still holding the computer. I glanced at the screen and reported, "We only have fifty-six minutes left."

I handed Jacob the time-travel computer, saying, "Let's go. June 1776. Philadelphia, Pennsylvania."

"Now that we are going back farther in time, I wish I knew some details about the actual history of the flag. I am afraid I might not be much help," Bo admitted as we waited for Jacob to reprogram the computer.

"It's okay, Bo," I said. "We'll just ask a lot of questions of the people we meet." Asking questions is my specialty.

"Done." Jacob cheered as he pulled the cartridge out of the back of the computer. The green glowing hole opened near the little desk where Bo had found the meeting room key.

"Have a nice trip," Zack said as he backed away from the time-travel hole. "I'll see you when you get back."

"What are you talking about?!" I turned to him. "You're coming with us."

"I told you I wasn't," Zack replied. "I'm not coming because I promised Mr. C that we wouldn't change history. I'm going to stay here and help William Canby."

I couldn't believe it. Zack is usually such a worrier.

Then again, Bo is usually so quiet. It was a crazy, mixed-up day.

"Hey, look," Jacob cried out. He was pointing at the time-travel hole. "It's shrinking."

The time-travel hole was getting smaller and smaller. Usually we like to hold hands as we jump, but now it was barely big enough for one person to fit through at a time.

"Let's just go," Jacob said, hovering over the hole. "Zack won't stay behind. He's too much of a bab— ooof!"

I shoved Jacob hard on his back. He fell down through the hole before he could insult his brother again. Insults were not going to get Zack to go with us.

Bo didn't know what to say, so he just jumped into the hole.

"Please come," I begged Zack. "We need you." It was true. "We're a team!" I insisted.

"Not today we aren't." Zack moved back three big steps from the time-travel hole. "See you later."

"Okay," I said sadly as I leaped into the rapidly closing time-travel hole. "See ya."

Betsy and George

It was a beautiful warm day. I made a nice soft landing on a patch of grass.

Zack landed on top of me.

"What are you doing here?" I asked him as I struggled to untangle my arms and legs from his.

Zack looked over and gave a mean look toward his brother. "I'm not a baby," he said firmly, "but I am a chicken." He gave a little laugh. "I really wanted to stay behind, but I got scared. What if something went wrong with the computer? I might have been stuck in 1870 forever." He was talking so fast, my ears could barely keep up. "I can't live in a time without television, cars, and, most important, junk food."

We both got up off the grass and headed over to

where Bo and Jacob were standing, looking surprised. "I'm glad you changed your mind," I told him.

"I didn't change my mind," Zack said, shaking his head. "I might be too scared to stay alone in 1870, but I still believe we are doing the wrong thing." He shot Bo and Jacob a fierce stare. "I'm fighting for Betsy Ross. While you look for evidence that someone else made the flag, I'm going to work my hardest to find proof that Betsy did it!"

"Well then," Jacob said with a wink, "since we aren't acting like one team today, let's act like two. It is me, Bo, Abigail, and the mystery flag maker versus the chicken and Betsy." Jacob laughed at his own joke. "Winning team gets to choose who speaks to the Historical Society of Pennsylvania in 1870."

This time, Zack wasn't insulted. Rather, he tucked his hands into his armpits and clucked proudly. "Let's hear it for Team Chicken." He punched the air. "Team Mystery's gonna take a lickin'!" Zack wiggled pretend tail feathers and did a fancy chicken dance.

I was sad that we weren't going to work together

like one team. Jacob said that when teammates dis-
agree, majority rules. I guess that only happens
sometimes. Other times, the team splits in two.

"Bummer," I said to myself. There was no point in
moping around, however. Even though we didn't all
agree, we still had work to do. We had to find out
who made the first American flag—fast.

We were standing across the street from a large
building. Careful not to be run over by a horse and
buggy, we hurried across the cobblestone road. The
sign in front of the building read CHRIST CHURCH.

"What day is it?" I asked Jacob.

Jacob studied the computer screen a second and
reported, "It's June 16, 1776. Since we didn't know
exactly what date we are looking for, I picked one at
random." Jacob smiled as he surveyed the area.
"We're going to have to ask around to see if anyone
knows who created the flag and then make another
jump to actually witness the event."

Zack puffed out his chest and announced, "I
already know who created the flag." At that, the
church's front doors opened and people began

pouring into the street. It was clearly Sunday. Religious services were just letting out.

"Excuse me," I said to the first man I saw. "We are looking for a flag maker."

"The only woman I am aware of who has a nearby upholstery shop is Betsy Ross," the man replied. "It was her husband's, John Ross's, store. He was a brave soldier, killed while helping to make America a free and independent country."

A young woman came up and joined the man. He tenderly put his arm around her, introduced her as his wife, and filled her in on the conversation. "Now Betsy Ross runs the upholstery shop," his wife put in. "I do not know if she has ever made a flag, but she sews just about everything else. Betsy Ross is a modern working woman! I think she is a true American heroine." Holding hands, the husband and wife casually strolled away.

"Ha!" Zack said, holding up one finger proudly. "That makes one point for Team Chicken. No points for Team Mystery."

"So Betsy Ross sews," Bo said without emotion.

"That doesn't mean she designed and created the first American flag."

"I get one point just because she sews," Zack said proudly. "That proves that Betsy *could* make a flag if someone asked her to."

As a man with a white powdered wig walked out of Christ Church, Zack declared, "Hey! Look, it's George Washington. That makes two points for me. None for you."

"How come you get a point for recognizing George Washington?" I asked Zack. "What's he got to do with Betsy and the flag?"

"Give him the point." Jacob sighed. "William Canby claimed that in 1776, George Washington visited Betsy Ross at her sewing shop. It was there he asked her to make the first flag."

"That's not proof," Bo countered. "So what if GW's in town? It doesn't mean he asked her to make the flag." GW was our time-traveling nickname for George Washington.

"It proves he *could* have asked her, right? Maybe he went to her shop just like William Canby said. If he wasn't in town, it wouldn't have been possible. But here he is! And"—Zack paused, carefully watching George Washington—"I think you'll agree that here comes my team's third point." Zack winked at us as a woman stepped out of the church and greeted George Washington.

"Who is that?" I asked, checking out her long dress and small white cap. She was carrying a large fabric bag. I could see knitting needles sticking out of the top.

Jacob shook his head. "I think that's Betsy Ross. She looks just like she does in that little painting on the back of our time-travel cartridge."

Zack got all excited. "That's definitely her! And she's talking to GW!"

"You don't get another point just because Betsy Ross knows George Washington!" Bo exclaimed. "It doesn't mean anything. Simply because they go to the same church doesn't mean she made the flag!"

"The way I see it, they *could* be talking about flags. That makes it three to nothing in favor of Betsy Ross sewing the first American flag." Zack held up three fingers on one hand and made an empty fist with the other. "Team Chicken is in the lead."

"Zack, your evidence is *not* proof," Bo protested. "Your points don't count! You can't just say that because she can sew, because GW is in town at the right time, and because Betsy knows George that Betsy Ross definitely made the flag." Bo's face was red. "To be a true historian, you need facts. Hard evidence. Historical documentation that shows without a doubt that Betsy Ross made the first American flag." Bo paused before adding, "It's just like the writer Mark Twain said: 'If it is a Miracle, any sort of evidence will answer, but if it is a Fact, proof is necessary.'"

"What kind of proof do we need?" I asked Bo.

"An order form signed by George Washington, or a receipt from the Continental Congress that shows she got paid for making the first flag. Maybe the drawing of the flag. Something like that," Bo answered. "Something written down that will last through time." Bo rolled his eyes at Zack. "So far, you have nothing."

Zack gave a goofy smile. He pointed at Bo, Jacob, and me, saying, "Actually, I have three points. You have nothing." His smile got bigger and goofier. "Plus, I have something else you don't have—the most important thing ever."

"What?" Jacob was baffled. "What could you possibly have that we don't have?"

"You don't even have a possible name for the mystery flag maker." Zack pointed straight ahead. "I have Betsy Ross!"

(6)

The Paper Star

"I'm going to go over there and ask her if she made the flag or not," Zack said as he hurried up the church steps toward Betsy. "That'll prove it for sure!"

"She might not tell the truth," Bo called after Zack as we hurried to keep up.

Zack stopped in his tracks and whipped his head around to face Bo. "Are you calling Betsy Ross a liar?"

Bo started to laugh. "Of course not. I just said that to get you to slow down."

Zack didn't think it was funny.

"Here's the thing," Bo told him. "William Canby says that Betsy Ross told him that she made the flag, right? The problem is that without the kind of historical evidence that I was telling you about, no one knows whether to believe his story."

"Are you saying it doesn't matter if Betsy Ross tells Zack she created the flag?" Jacob asked.

"It'll matter to Zack," Bo told us. "But in the future, if there isn't an old receipt or a drawing or something, no one will be able to prove the story is true. It's like the historian David Thelen wrote: 'The challenge of history is to recover the past and introduce it to the present.'"

Zack's face fell slightly as he considered Bo's words. "Okay," he admitted at last. "I'm not giving back my team's three points, but I'll keep looking for some hard evidence."

Bo then turned to me, saying, "Can you ask around to find out if there is another, different flag maker in town? I'm hoping to discover someone who has a drawing or receipt proving they made the first flag instead of Betsy Ross."

"I'll ask her." I chose a girl a little older than us. I figured she was about eleven. She was busy climbing up a tree by the side of the church.

By the time we got over to the tree, the girl had reached a high branch and was scooting out on a thick limb. "Hey," I called out. "Do you know anyone round here who makes flags?"

"Sure," the girl called back at me. "My aunt makes flags."

"Does she have a shop in town?" I asked.

"Yes." She pointed down the street. "My aunt lives and works at 239 Arch Street."

"Does she know George Washington?" Zack asked, defending his three points.

"Of course," the girl answered. "Our family church pew is right next to his."

"Drat," Zack muttered. "Maybe there is another possible flag maker after all."

The girl reached into her dress pocket and pulled out a piece of paper. "Want to see something amazing?" she asked us. "It has to do with flags."

"Sure," I said. "Toss it down." I wondered what she was holding.

"I do not want to," she replied. "I enjoy sitting up here. You must come up if you want to see it." The

girl cupped her hand around the piece of paper so we couldn't peek.

There was no way we'd all fit on that tree branch. As curious as I was to see what she was holding, I didn't want to go up there. Besides, I was wearing CeCe's cowboy boots. They were perfect for riding horses or just looking cool, but not for climbing trees.

I looked over at Zack to see if he was willing to go instead. "What if the branch snaps?" he asked me, full of worry. "What if I break my arm? Do they even have doctors in 1776? X-ray machines? Plaster casts?"

Jacob looked down at the computer screen. "We only have forty-two minutes," he reported. "I'll go up the tree." Jacob grabbed the tree like he was hugging it and began to shimmy up. When he reached the lowest branch, he called up, "Can you show me whatever you've got from here?"

"No," the girl replied. "If you're interested in flags, you have to come all the way up."

Jacob kept climbing, slowly at first, then faster as he

found good places to put his feet. When he reached the thick branch, he scooted across, just like we'd seen the girl do. The branch shook slightly under the weight of the two kids. A few leaves fell to the ground.

"Be careful," I called up at Jacob.

Jacob took the paper from the girl and held it up. It was a star.

"Three members of a Continental Committee came to my aunt's store and asked her to make a star-spangled banner." The girl went on with her story while Jacob looked at the paper star. "The committee wanted a square flag, with thirteen red and white stripes and thirteen randomly placed six-pointed stars on a blue background." Even though she was talking to Jacob, she was telling the story loud enough for us all to hear. "There are thirteen colonies, you know."

We all nodded.

"My aunt told the committee that the flag should be one third longer than its width. That the stars should be in a circle. And that the stars should have five points instead of six. She even drew them a new sketch of what the flag should look like." The girl gave a small laugh. "One of the members of the committee said he thought it was too difficult to make a five-pointed star!"

As the girl laughed some more, the tree branch shook wildly. I watched Jacob grab on to the limb above him, holding on for his life.

"Then she showed them exactly how to cut a five-pointed star." The girl took the star back from Jacob and held it up so we could all see it.

"Cool," I said. Turning to Bo, I asked, "Is that star proof enough that her aunt made the flag?"

"It might be," Bo said, rubbing his chin and considering the possibility. "It's not the best proof, because it doesn't have a date on it, or a signature. But it is a really good story. I wonder what the lady's name is?"

"Hey," I called up to the girl. "Who's your au—" The rest of my question was drowned out by the sound of breaking wood. The tree branch cracked straight through.

"Ahhh!" cried the girl as she tumbled to the ground.

"Ahhh!" cried Jacob as he fell after her.

First Zack had fallen on me as we traveled through time. Now it was his brother Jacob's turn.

We were both knocked flat to the ground. Luckily, we were both fine. The girl landed on the soft grass next to us.

"Margaret, are you hurt?" A man came running over from the church.

"I am fine, Mr. Wetherill," she answered, picking herself up and dusting off her dress.

"What is this?" Mr. Wetherill asked, reaching for the paper and plucking it off the ground.

"It's a paper star," Margaret answered.

"Ah yes, your aunt just told me the story about the committee and the flag." Mr. Wetherill studied the star in his hand. "This is very important. I would like to hold it for safekeeping."

"Certainly," Margaret told him. "You may take it. I will simply ask my aunt to cut me another."

While Mr. Wetherill walked away, he was still looking at the star. Margaret turned to wave good-bye to us before she also disappeared down the street.

I realized that in the excitement of the tree branch breaking, we'd forgotten to find out her aunt's name. "Darn," I said. "We might have just lost our chance to find out the name of the first flag maker."

"So what if Margaret has a paper star?" Zack said. "It doesn't mean anything. I still believe that Betsy Ross created the first flag." Zack was rubbing his chin, just like Bo does when he's thinking really hard. "Wait a second! When we were in 1870, didn't William Canby say something about Betsy Ross having a receipt for naval standards dated May 1777? We could pop over there and check out her receipt. That would be really good historic proof!"

"All that receipt shows is that a year from now, Betsy Ross made a bunch of flags for the navy," Bo said. "That receipt doesn't mean anything. It still doesn't prove she sewed the first American flag." I could tell that Bo was still wondering about the woman who made the paper star.

"Then again," Jacob put in, "May 1777 was one of the dates Mr. C put on the blackboard." Jacob reminded us, "He must have thought that the receipt was important." The way Jacob said it, I wondered if he was starting to think about joining Team Chicken.

"It's just a receipt for a bunch of flags," Bo remarked. "It's not important at all. Let's jump ahead to the next date on Mr. C's blackboard time line." Bo was smiling again.

"Where are we going?" I asked. I closed my eyes and concentrated, but no matter how hard I tried I couldn't picture the blackboard.

"May 25, 1780." Bo seemed very pleased with himself. He asked Jacob to set the computer to take us there. "I think I solved the mystery of Margaret's aunt." Bo was full of excitement. "William Canby said that some people believe Francis Hopkinson made the first flag in 1780." Bo rubbed his chin so hard he was making a red spot under his lower lip. "I never heard of Francis Hopkinson, but I bet that she's the one who made the star. Maybe she has a receipt, or that drawing Margaret said she made for the Continental Committee."

If Jacob had been considering a switch to Team Chicken, he was solidly back on Team Mystery.

"Let's go see if we can find Francis Hopkinson," Jacob agreed as he pressed a bunch of buttons on the front of the computer. With only thirty-five minutes left on the computer timer, Jacob opened the green hole right next to us in the grass. "Maybe we can give Francis Hopkinson back her place in American history!" he exclaimed.

"I am certain that Betsy Ross made the first American flag," Zack said, walking slowly to the edge of the hole. "So I'm only coming because I don't want to be left behind in 1776, either." He clucked like a chicken and jumped into the hole.

I jumped through time with Jacob and Bo right behind me. As I fell through the swirling green mist, I distinctly heard Bo call out, "Team Mystery is now called Team Hopkinson! We are about to make a million-point comeback."

7

Francis Hopkinson

Francis Hopkinson was not Margaret's aunt. I was now positive because Francis Hopkinson wasn't a woman. She was a man. I mean, he was a man. Apparently Francis was a popular boy's name in the 1700s.

We found this out not because we met Mr. Hopkinson. No, he wasn't around. But there was a huge painted portrait of him hanging on the wall in his office. In the picture he was sitting at a desk, holding a quill pen thoughtfully in his hand.

"Drat. I wish I knew more about the history of the American flag," Bo moaned. "I should have at least known that Francis Hopkinson was a guy." I knew

Bo was feeling bad. He's usually the one with all the facts on our adventures.

"It doesn't matter that Francis Hopkinson wasn't Margaret's aunt," I said, trying to make Bo feel better. "This place and date were on Mr. C's time line. And William Canby specifically mentioned Francis Hopkinson, so he must be important." I looked around at the small office we'd landed in. "Let's find out what's up."

"Tick tock," Zack reminded us. He glanced over Jacob's shoulder at the computer screen. "We're going to need to save enough time to get back to 1870 in time to help William Canby give his speech." Zack held up three fingers reminding us of the team scores so far.

"We aren't going back until we learn more about Francis Hopkinson," Jacob told Zack. "We're still not certain that William Canby is giving a speech today!" He looked at me. "Abigail might be giving a new version."

"She's not saying anything." Zack took a big step

toward his brother. "William Canby is going to give his speech!"

"You don't know that." Jacob leaned in toward Zack.

I jumped between them. "Knock it off," I instructed. "There's no time to argue."

The boys each stepped back, but I could tell they were still itching for a fight.

The office we were standing in was small, but a big window made the room bright and cheery. There was a polished wood desk in the middle with papers scattered in big piles all over the place.

Jacob moved to the side to check out a large bookcase stuffed with so many books and papers that they were hanging off the shelves. He pulled out a rumpled sheet of parchment. "Hey," Jacob called to us after he scanned the writing. "This is a short biography about Francis Hopkinson. He wasn't just a flag maker. Now he lives in Philadelphia, but he signed the Declaration of Independence on behalf of New Jersey. It also says that he composed music."

Jacob handed the paper to Zack. "Wow," Zack said when he finished reading. "Francis Hopkinson was really important in the Continental Congress. He was the Treasurer of Loans for the newly established American government."

Zack handed the parchment back to Jacob, saying, "Of course, nothing in this biography proves that Francis Hopkinson designed the first American flag."

"Ah," said a deep male voice in the doorway, "but I did design the flag."

We all snapped our heads around to find Francis Hopkinson standing in the doorway.

My face was burning hot. We'd just been caught snooping around the office of a really important man in United States history. I was really embarrassed. "I'm so sorry," I told him. As it turned out, I didn't really have to apologize. He was really nice.

"Can I help you with something?" Francis Hopkinson asked us. Then, looking over his shoulder out the office door, he said, "How did you get in here? Mrs. Templeton is a very strict assistant. She rarely lets anyone come in without an appointment. Even my wife is afraid to come to the office unannounced."

Jacob laughed, hiding the time-travel computer in

his pocket as he spoke. "We just popped in."

Francis Hopkinson smiled. "Well then, it must be important business if you snuck past Mrs. Templeton. How can I be of service?"

I looked to Bo to explain why we'd come. By the expression on his face, it was clear he wasn't about to talk. He was doing great speaking loudly to us today, even to Mr. C, but when it came to talking to anyone else, his mouth was glued shut as usual.

I took charge. "We came to talk about the flag," I told Francis Hopkinson.

He grinned. "Well then, you came at just the right time. I was about to send a letter." He went over to his desk and sifted through a stack of papers. Parchment fragments fell to the floor as he glanced through each sheet, searching for the one he wanted. "Aha!" he exclaimed when he discovered the letter at the bottom of the pile. He also pulled out a drawing on a smaller piece of paper.

Francis Hopkinson handed the letter to Jacob and the drawing to me.

"This is a letter asking for payment," Jacob

explained after he finished reading. "Sort of like a receipt." Jacob passed the letter to Bo.

Bo finished the letter and handed it back to Francis Hopkinson, although he still wouldn't talk directly to the man. "This letter is asking the Continental Congress to pay Francis Hopkinson for the design of the United States flag, a continental currency, a seal for the Admiralty and Treasury Boards, and a Great Seal for the United States." He paused, then added, "Francis Hopkinson calls them 'labours of fancy.'"

"You've been busy!" I exclaimed. "That's a lot of stuff you did."

"I have been working hard for a new, independent America," Francis Hopkinson replied. He turned to Jacob and Bo, saying, "Did you notice I did not ask for money?"

"The letter says that you wanted to be paid with a quarter cask of wine," Bo muttered.

"I don't think it is too much to ask," Francis Hopkinson told us. "We are a poor, new nation. I will gladly take the payment in wine as a token of gratitude."

Bo was excited. "This letter is the exact kind of hard evidence we've been looking for." Bo held up all his fingers and flashed them over and over at Zack. "That makes a million points for Team Hopkinson, three points for Team Chicken."

Bo turned to Jacob. "We can go now. Abigail has a speech to make to the Historical Society of Pennsylvania."

"What about Margaret's aunt's story?" Zack gave Bo a bitter stare.

"We have no clue who her aunt is, and Margaret doesn't have any real proof!" Bo told Zack.

Proof. Hmmm. I thought about Margaret's aunt and the story of the five-pointed star. "Can we see your flag design?" I asked Francis Hopkinson. I was totally curious what his flag looked like. I remembered that Margaret had said that her aunt's flag was thirteen red and white stripes, with thirteen stars in a circle on a blue background.

"I already gave it to your friend." Francis Hopkinson indicated the parchment paper in Zack's hand.

"I almost forgot," Zack said, glancing down at the

paper. He held the drawing up for us all to see. The flag design had thirteen red and white stripes representing the thirteen colonies. A small blue box in the upper left corner had thirteen white stars. The stars were in rows, not a circle.

The flag was almost identical to the one we fly today, only we have more stars. We are up to fifty states, compared to the thirteen colonies in 1780. As far as proof went, it looked like Bo was right and Team Hopkinson was in the lead—way in the lead.

"How did you come up with this design?" I asked Francis Hopkinson.

"A few years ago," he explained, "on June 14, 1777, the first flag resolution was passed. Congress declared exactly what they would like the flag to look like."

"I know this!" Bo suddenly chimed in. "I read about it in a book once. Because it was fact! The flag resolution said, 'Resolved. That the flag of the United States be thirteen stripes alternate red and white, that the Union be thirteen stars white in a blue field

representing a new constellation.'" Bo was pretty excited to have added to the conversation. I think it made him feel better to finally know something about flags.

"Oh, come on," Zack groaned. "You have to give back half of your million points. It's totally possible that the flag resolution describes the flag that was already made by Betsy Ross, not one that was about to be created by Francis Hopkinson."

Zack had a good argument there. Betsy Ross would have made the flag before the resolution. Francis Hopkinson would have made his after Congress had already described the flag. My head was starting to spin. I couldn't decide who I thought had really made the flag.

"Hang on a second," Zack said, studying the Hopkinson flag design. "Can you make a five-pointed star?"

Francis Hopkinson handed me a stack full of different kinds of flag designs. I flipped through the pages. They all had six-pointed stars. "European designs all have six-pointed stars. Why would I want to make a five-pointed star?"

"Because that's the kind of star that is on the American flag," Zack replied, not looking at Francis Hopkinson, but staring at me and Bo and Jacob as he said it.

"I'm just asking because I am curious," I said, "but do you know anyone around here who might make flags with five-pointed stars?"

"I heard Betsy Ross was playing with her scissors," he laughed. "But she didn't design the flag, if that's what you want to know. I did."

Hmm. Now I wasn't so sure. Yes, Francis Hopkinson had written a letter asking the Continental Congress to pay him for a flag design. Like Bo had been telling us, we needed proof and that was pretty good proof.

Then again, his design was created from what he read in the flag resolution of 1777 and his stars were the wrong kind.

Then again . . .

I was getting a terrible headache.

That's when it came to me. I turned to Francis

Hopkinson. "Did you just say that Betsy Ross was playing with her scissors? Do you mean she made a five-pointed star?"

"That's what people say," he told me. "There is a legend that George Washington went to her and showed her a flag design. She did not like the six-pointed star and quickly cut a five-pointed one." He went on talking, but I stopped listening.

"Zack," I said quietly, not to interrupt the story that Francis Hopkinson was now telling to just Bo and Jacob, since they were the only ones still paying attention. "Can I join Team Chicken?"

Zack looked at me oddly. "What about getting hard evidence? What about Francis Hopkinson's letter?"

"I don't need hard evidence. Just now I made a decision about who I think created the first flag." I shrugged. "Margaret's aunt made a flag with a five-pointed star, just like the stars on the flags we fly today," I told him. "I saw the star. That was all the evidence I need."

"How does that paper star prove to you that Betsy Ross made the flag?" Zack asked.

"Margaret's aunt must be Betsy Ross." I smiled. "When we were in 1870, William Canby said that he had a paper signed by Margaret Donaldson Boggs saying that her aunt, Elizabeth Claypoole, created the 'first star-spangled banner'!"

"Abigail, you are a regular Nancy Drew!" Zack exclaimed.

Suddenly a woman stuck her head in the office door. "Mr. Hopkinson, you have an appointment waiting."

"Thank you, Mrs. Templeton," Francis Hopkinson replied, then quickly asked the boys to give him back the letter and drawing. "I must go," he said. "Since you popped into my office, I expect that you can simply pop out again." And with that, he left us standing near his desk.

"I just joined Team Chicken." I told Jacob and Bo that I was giving up the search for hard evidence. "I like Margaret Donaldson Boggs's story about her aunt and the five-pointed star." I was jazzed up and ready to go to 1870 again.

"But, Abigail," Jacob reminded me, "Francis

Hopkinson says he designed the flag himself. You heard him say it."

I shrugged. "The truth is, I don't know who really created it. Maybe Betsy Ross really did make the five-pointed stars. Maybe Francis Hopkinson designed it." I sighed. "I'll never know the answer. So I have to go with my gut on this one. I decided that Betsy Ross played an important role in the creation of the flag. She'll lose her place in American history if we don't get back there and let William Canby give his speech."

"I suppose I'm switching to Team Chicken too." Jacob apologized to Bo. "We just can't get the hard evidence to prove that someone else made the flag. I think Abigail and Zack are right; it's time to make a decision." He checked the computer. "We have twenty-two minutes to make sure history stays the way it was written."

Apparently Zack and Jacob weren't going to fight after all. Jacob gave his brother a big high five.

"Doesn't anyone care if the Betsy Ross story is a myth?" Bo asked. "You all are going to let her have her place in our history books for something she might not have done?"

"Until we are proven wrong," I said. "Betsy Ross did a lot of good for America. Why not let her keep her story?"

Bo thought about it for about a second. "Fine. Just peachy." Bo put his hands on his hips. "Go ahead and jump through time, but I'm staying here. I'm going to help Francis Hopkinson get his rightful place in history as the man who designed the first American flag."

"Oh, come on, Bo," Jacob groaned. "He might have a drawing and a receipt, but he's . . ." Jacob paused to do the math. "The flag was made in 1776. Now it's 1780." He counted quickly. "He's too late. Abigail, Zack, and I all agree that Betsy Ross deserves to be known as the person who created the flag. We need to hang together now and finish this mission. Don't be such a baby because you were outvoted."

"I'm not a baby," Bo countered. "Take it back." Bo stepped forward toward Jacob with his fists clenched.

This all seemed very familiar. Too familiar. "Boys!"

I put myself between them. "We're wasting time! We'll never be able to help William Canby and Betsy Ross if we don't hurry. Let's go," I said. "May 25, 1870. Philadelphia, Pennsylvania." Jacob set up the computer and the green hole opened in the middle of Francis Hopkinson's office.

"Have a nice trip," Bo said as he backed away from the time-travel hole.

"Let's just go," Jacob said, hovering over the hole. "Bo won't really stay behind. He knows we aren't coming back here—ever."

I looked at Bo. Was he so committed to Francis Hopkinson's version of history that he was willing to risk being left behind? Jacob thought he was bluffing. I wasn't so sure. . . .

"Please come," I begged. "We're a team!" Jacob and Zack jumped into the hole without Bo.

"Not today we aren't." Bo moved back three big steps from the time-travel hole. "See you later."

"Okay," I said sadly as I leaped into the rapidly closing time-travel hole. "See ya."

(8)

Sam Wetherill

I landed on the hardwood floor outside the room where the Historical Society of Pennsylvania was meeting.

Bo landed on top of me. I was seriously starting to wish I'd brought a helmet for protection today.

"What are you doing here?" I asked him as I struggled to untangle my arms and legs from his.

He looked at Jacob. "I'm not a baby. And I wasn't scared to stay in 1780." As we got up, Bo stood still for a second and rubbed his chin. This time his forehead wasn't wrinkled. He was thinking. Just plain old thinking, not plotting or planning. "After weighing the evidence, I cannot prove who made the first American flag. I don't know for sure if it was Francis Hopkinson. Or Betsy Ross.

"I once read that when there is no real historical proof, the next and last resort then of the historian is tradition. When I really thought about those words, I realized Betsy Ross and her story *are* the tradition. She's our American tradition." Bo closed his eyes. "The weirdest thing is that for the first time in my life, I simply can't remember where I read that great piece of wisdom!"

I thought Bo was done speaking, but then he said, "I realized something else, too."

"What?" I asked. I was feeling another quote coming on.

"Helen Keller said, 'Alone we can do so little; together we can do so much.'" Bo grinned.

"Does that mean we should act like a team?" I asked. Finally we were going to work together, just the way we were supposed to!

"Yeah." Bo shook his head and shrugged. "I suppose I am coming over to Team Chicken too."

"Let's hear it for Team Chicken!" Zack tucked his arms under his pits and clucked wildly.

"Babs Magee is gonna take a lickin'!" Bo finished the rhyme. Then he started clucking too.

"Speaking of Babs," I said, "we better let everyone out of the meeting room and help William Canby give his speech. Our adventure time is nearly finished."

I turned around to unlock the meeting room door.

"Oh, no!" I exclaimed. "The door . . . it's gone!"

"It's not gone," Zack corrected. He pointed down by our feet. There were wooden splinters and big chunks of the door scattered across the floor.

Bo reached down near his feet and picked up the brass doorknob.

Jacob found an ax leaning against a side wall. "I think Team Chicken is in trouble," Jacob remarked, looking at the empty room.

My head was racing. Where would everyone have gone?

Suddenly I heard a bang from inside the meeting room.

"Are you certain the room is empty?" I turned to Bo.

"I don't see anyone," Bo replied.

We all stepped into the meeting room together. When we heard the noise again, this time it was more like a slam and a kick than a bang. Then there was a crash, like metal pails falling off a shelf.

"That's probably just a cat," Zack added, looking a bit scared. "Or a dog. But it might be a bear." Under his breath he muttered, "Did they have bears in Philadelphia in 1870?"

Jacob, Bo, and I followed the sounds. They were coming from behind a closed door at the far end of the room. Zack was tiptoeing very cautiously behind us. "Be careful," he warned. "Some bears eat people."

I looked back over my shoulder at him. "Bears don't eat people. They eat berries and fish, maybe an occasional seal."

Zack blushed. "I'm just saying, bears can be dangerous."

Zack was right about bears, but when the bang

happened a third time and a voice shouted, "Ouch!" we knew it wasn't a bear.

I quickly reached out toward the doorknob. There was someone behind that door. And he was hurt. We had to help.

The door was locked. "Drat," I muttered.

"Is someone there?" a man called out from inside the closet. "Have you come to rescue me?"

"We'll get you out," I replied. I grabbed the doorknob and tugged hard. It wouldn't budge.

"I have another quote about teamwork," Bo said as he grabbed me around my waist. "Margaret Carty said, 'The nice thing about teamwork is that you always have others on your side.'" We pulled on the door together. It still wouldn't open.

"I have a quote," Jacob said as he put his arms around Bo's waist. "The father of modern computing, Bill Gates, once said, 'We're only at the beginning of what we have to do here.'" The three of us pulled on the door together, but still, the door stayed locked shut.

With a giggle, Zack wrapped his arms around his

brother. "In the video game Kingdom Hearts, Sora says, 'Although my heart may be weak, it's not alone. My friends are my power!'"

It was just like Zack to quote a video game character instead of a real person. "That one wins the quote-of-the-day award," I told Zack with a laugh.

Working as a team, we managed to snap the hinges and pop open the door. We all jumped back as a mop clattered to the ground. Then a pail crashed onto the floor. Finally a man tumbled out.

I recognized him immediately. He was still clutching his speech in his hand.

"William Canby!" I exclaimed. "What are you doing locked in a closet?"

"That insane woman wearing a yellow hat locked me in," he replied, dusting off his suit and straightening his hat. "She shoved me into the closet, then broke down the meeting room door and insisted everyone follow her." He smoothed out the wrinkled pages of his speech. "She claims that she has evidence that she created the first American flag."

Suddenly my Nancy Drew-ness kicked in for the second time today. The last date written on Mr. C's blackboard was 1925. Babs had said that something would be found in 1925 in a safe at Sam Wetherill's home, but that she could show it to everyone today. Whatever it was, Babs thought that it would prove she made the first flag instead of Betsy Ross.

"They're following Babs to Sam Wetherill's house." I quickly asked Mr. Canby if he knew where Mr. Wetherill lived. He did and agreed to lead us there.

"We've jumped through time. We've searched and searched for real, hard evidence. We all know that there is no historic proof determining who actually made the first flag!" Bo was clearly baffled. "I can't imagine what Babs thinks she is going to show everyone."

Jacob told us to hurry. "We only have eighteen minutes left on the computer."

Zack groaned, whining, "I told Mr. C we needed more time, but *noooo*. He said this was going to be easy. He said we wouldn't even need our usual two hours."

I grabbed Zack's arm. "You're going to have to whine and walk at the same time." I tugged him along.

We knew where to go and what we had to do.

It was time to stop Babs Magee.

⑨

Sam Wetherill's Safe

Speeding along in William Canby's horse-drawn buggy, we arrived at Sam Wetherill's house with nine minutes to go. The house was on a farm at the end of a long lane. I saw goats, sheep, and a chicken coop as we hurried past.

"We are cutting this waaay too close," Zack muttered as we rushed up to the front of the house. "There is no waaay we can find Babs Magee, make her stop, and get everyone back to the Historical Society meeting in just nine minutes."

Zack was right. There just wasn't enough time. We were going to have to find a quick and easy way to stop Babs Magee. The rest . . . well, we'd have to hope that William Canby could take care of setting history back on track.

I turned to William Canby. "We will get rid of the insane woman in the yellow hat. After that it'll be up to you to get everyone back to the meeting." I pointed at the papers he still carried in his hand. "It's really important that you give your speech today."

William Canby nodded. He'd do his part. Now we just had to do ours.

The five of us hurried to the front door. William Canby reached for the knob. "Not another locked door!" he exclaimed after testing the knob and finding that it wouldn't budge.

"We could try using teamwork again." Jacob suggested that he'd hold the knob this time and the rest of us could grab on to him.

"Or we could just go in through that open window," Zack said, pointing to a low window near the side of the front door. The window was so near to the ground, we wouldn't even need boosting.

"You're a genius," I told Zack as I stood beneath the windowsill.

"You should probably stay out here," Jacob suggested to William Canby, "just in case anyone tries to go out the front. You can stop them and convince them to go back to the meeting room."

William Canby agreed. "I want to thank you children for helping me. From this day forward, all Americans will know who really made that first American flag."

I immediately saw Bo roll his eyes. I was worried he'd lose his head again and start screaming, "NOOOO! IT'S A MYTH!" But he didn't.

Very calmly, Bo said, "There isn't any proof that Betsy Ross made the first flag, you know."

"Yes, I know," said William Canby. "As I will say in my speech, it was thought advisable to make a search amongst the national archives, and also in the published *Journal of Congress,* and in all other works likely to have any reference or bearing upon the subject, in the hope that some official testimony might be obtained to establish the truth . . . for it is only the truth that the real student of history is striving to reach. . . ."

At that, Bo smiled.

William Canby continued, "The most careful and searching inquiry was accordingly made of the printed works referred to, in fact of every book, pamphlet, or newspaper in the Philadelphia Library, and in this and other libraries, that would be likely to throw any light upon the subject. . . . The search was fruitless, as might have been expected, as to the finding of any matter throwing light on the origin of the design, and the making of the flag."

"Well then," I interrupted. "If there is no proof, how can you say that your grandmother, Betsy Ross, made the flag?"

William Canby flipped through the pages of his speech and recited, "The next and the last resort then of the historian is tradition."

"That's where I read it!" Bo exclaimed. "A few years ago, I read William Canby's speech. When I discovered there was no historical proof for the creation of the flag, I gave up on Betsy Ross." He looked over at William Canby, adding, "But now I understand, sometimes there are facts, and sometimes there is tradition. History is made of both." Bo's face looked completely at peace. He didn't need to rub his chin anymore. And there wasn't even a single wrinkle on his forehead.

We said good-bye and good luck to William Canby.

And he said the same to us as, one by one, we swung our legs over the windowsill and dropped into the Wetherills' home.

Voices were coming from the room next door. Lots of voices. And above them all I heard Babs Magee.

We snuck into the back of the crowded room, hunching low so Babs wouldn't see us. She was standing in the middle of the room. A table was in front of her. On the table was a footlocker.

"Whew." Zack sighed. He whispered, "We made it in time! What should we do?"

I shrugged. Sure, we'd gotten there before Babs had opened the locker, but what now?

"Inside this locker is my proof," Babs announced to the gathering. She bent low to look at the lock on the box. Then she lifted her head and said to Samuel Wetherill's grandson, "Do you have the key?"

He told Babs that he'd have to go get the key. He walked away. The crowd was brimming with excitement again. They really believed that whatever was in that locker would prove that Babs Magee had made the first flag.

"Let's hear it for Team Chicken," Jacob suddenly whispered. I glanced at him. He had a seriously enormous grin on his face.

"Babs Magee is gonna take a lickin'," I finished. Then I knew exactly what to do. So did Zack. And Bo. "Jacob," I said. "Forget about Zack, you're the real genius!"

"We're twins," Zack reminded me. "We can both be geniuses."

I laughed.

Staying low, we hurried back into the first room and back out the window.

Zack is the fastest runner in the third grade. He

told the rest of us to wait. He'd be right back.

He was off in a blur as he ran down the lane to the animal pens. A few seconds later Zack came back with a chicken tucked under each arm. He handed one to me and one to Bo. Then he disappeared again. This time he gave a chicken to Jacob and kept the last one for himself.

"Let's hear it for Team Chicken!" Zack patted his bird on the head before swinging himself back over the windowsill and into the Wetherills' house.

We each repeated the cheer as we followed him in.

Luckily, Mr. Wetherill hadn't come back with the locker key yet.

It was time to cause a distraction. And we were going to make a big one.

I gave my chicken a good-luck kiss on the beak and set her free. She started clucking loudly and flapping her wings. People from the Historical Society looked down and were surprised to see a chicken loose in the house. They were even more surprised to see two chickens. And then three.

At four chickens, they weren't surprised anymore.

They were freaking out! Everyone was rushing around, shouting, and trying to catch the chickens.

My chicken flew up to a candle chandelier and refused to come down. She was happy sitting there, clucking at the people below.

Bo's chicken was on a bookcase, too high up for anyone to reach.

Zack's chicken was dashing around the floor, running from person to person, narrowly escaping the hands that were trying to catch her.

And Jacob's chicken had found the best resting place of all. In all the excitement, Babs Magee had tripped and fallen onto the floor. Jacob's chicken was now standing on her chest. Her wings were flapping in Babs's eyes. She kept leaning down and pecking at Babs's front coat pocket. If I didn't know better, I'd have sworn that chicken was looking for Babs Magee's time-travel computer.

"Let's hear it for Team Chicken!" I called out loud and clear above the crowd. Bo, Jacob, Zack, and I scampered to the front of the room. Not only was Zack a fast runner, but he'd been in the weight-lifting club at school. He grabbed the trunk and we followed him at light speed back out the window and down to the chicken coop.

Safely inside, Zack tried to put his spy-club skills to work opening the trunk. "I wish I hadn't quit after just one meeting," he moaned. "They were working on cracking codes that week. If only I'd have gone to the picking locks meeting instead."

"That's all right, Zack," I comforted him. "I have an idea." I told him to put the trunk on the ground. "Good thing I wore CeCe's cowboy boots today," I said as I gave the trunk a swift kick in the side. The lid popped open.

I winked at the boys. "I bet you all thought I was just wearing these boots because they looked nice." I smiled.

I leaned over the trunk. There was so much junk in it—old junk: a bottle of ink and a quill, a child's doll, a silver spoon. I took out each item and carefully set it on the ground of the chicken coop. The stuff in this trunk was already almost a hundred years old. I didn't want to destroy anything.

"We have three minutes," Jacob warned me. He held up the computer, ready to open the time-travel hole to take us home. "Maybe we should forget about whatever's in there." He pointed at the trunk. "As long as Babs Magee doesn't have the trunk, she doesn't have whatever proof she needed to show that she made the flag. Now that we stole her proof, I bet she's already time-traveled away."

"She's probably on to the next famous American on Mr. C's list," Zack added. "I wish we could stop her for good!"

"Someday we will," Bo put in. He leaned down next to me. "I'd really like to know what proof she thought she had," Bo said. He reached into the trunk and pulled out a small tin box. It was the last thing inside the trunk. I put back the other things while Bo examined the box.

"Two minutes," Jacob reported. "We've gotta go."

"Just give me another second," Bo said as he struggled to open the lid on the small tin. He twisted a tiny knob and lifted the lid. Inside was a piece of folded paper.

Bo tenderly held the paper in his hand. He didn't need to unfold it. We all already knew what it was. But Bo wanted to be sure. He lifted one corner at a time, until the whole paper was laid out flat in his hand.

"Betsy Ross's star," Zack said, awe in his voice. "It's the paper star that Betsy Ross used to show George Washington that she could make five-pointed stars."

"Samuel Wetherill took it home." I took the star from Bo and began to fold it back up.

"He saved it all this time." Jacob looked amazed.

Bo took the folded star back from me, put it into the tin box, and replaced the tin into the trunk, closing the lid with a bang.

Then he stood up. Bo asked Jacob to grab one end of the trunk and help him drag it to a small storage room in the chicken coop. The two of them put the trunk up on the highest shelf they could find. Zack and I stacked bags of chicken feed in front of the trunk, hiding it from view.

"The star itself isn't hard evidence," Bo said as we walked outside. "But it is super cool!"

At that, the computer began to beep.

"Five seconds," Jacob told us. He pulled the cartridge out of the computer.

The green time-travel hole opened between the chicken coop and the goat pen. I could still hear the chickens we'd let loose clucking inside the Wetherills' home. I could also see William Canby standing on the front stoop, just where we'd left him, waiting for the crowd to follow him back to the Historical Society meeting. I'd have waved, but he was looking down at his speech. He was probably practicing one last time before he gave it for real.

Jacob, Zack, Bo, and I gathered around the time-travel hole. We held hands.

On the count of three we jumped, and on four we landed, because time travel is really fast.

⑩

Home Again

We fell onto the school soccer fields. And for the first time all day, no one landed on top of me. Instead, I landed on top of Mr. C.

I apologized, but he just laughed. "I'm glad to see you. I came outside to look for you kids because I was starting to worry. It should have been such an easy mission." He looked suspiciously over at Bo. "What took you so long?"

Zack quickly said, "This was the easiest mission we ever had." I had to bite my tongue to keep myself from laughing.

"It was so easy," Jacob added, "we decided to hang around and learn as much as we could about Betsy Ross and the American flag."

"And did you learn something interesting?" Mr. C still had that curious look on his face.

I was about to tell Mr. C what I learned when Bo piped up. "I sure did," Bo said softly. He was back to being the quiet, shy kid we all knew so well.

We had to lean in to hear while Bo told Mr. C the truth about our mission. He explained how he thought he could set history straight by finding the true creator of the first American flag. He was completely honest about our journeys through the green hole, following the dates on Mr. C's time line. Bo even told Mr. C that Babs Magee thought she could use the paper star as proof that she met with George Washington and made the first flag.

"We hid the locker with the paper star in it," Jacob added.

"I'm not sure if the Wetherills really found the locker in the chicken coop. The important part is that we hid it so well, no one should discover it until 1925," Zack put in. "We also made sure that William Canby was able to give his speech, putting Betsy Ross back in our textbooks." He punched the air, like a cheer. "Everything is back just the way it is supposed to be."

"We tried, but we never found out who really made the flag," Bo admitted.

"So, if you didn't find a mystery flag maker, what did you learn from your investigation?" Mr. C asked Bo.

"French artist and writer Jean Cocteau once said, 'History becomes legend and legend becomes history,'" Bo replied.

"I'm not sure what you mean." Mr. C challenged Bo to explain.

Bo rubbed his chin for a second, then answered. "I suppose it means that history is about way more than just facts." Bo shrugged. "Even if it is a myth, Betsy Ross and the story of the flag is still an important part of American history."

Mr. C proudly put his hand on top of Bo's head and ruffled his hair. "You learned an important lesson today."

Jacob gave Mr. C back the time-travel computer. It was time to go home.

"I learned something too," I said as we walked together off the soccer fields. "All day long Bo's been giving us quotes from famous writers and great thinkers. Jacob and Zack shared quotes too. I haven't said one quote all day." I stopped and put my hands on my hips. "Until now."

Everyone quit moving and turned to look at me.

"On a poster in my dad's office at work is a quote that I've never really understood until today." I thought about the poster. I didn't want to mess up any of the words. "Henry Ford once said, 'Coming together is a beginning. Keeping together is progress. Working together is success.'"

Now I understood that Henry Ford's words were totally true. Sure, today Jacob, Zack, Bo, and I had gone on a time-travel adventure together, but that was just the beginning. Keeping together was more difficult. And working together, well, we didn't act like a team until nearly the end of our adventure.

As I thought about our History Club adventure, I smiled.

We might not have found out who made the first flag, but according to Henry Ford, today was definitely a success.

A huge, enormous, massive, gigantic, wonderful success.

Let's hear it for Team Chicken!

Cluck.

A Letter to Our Readers

Dear Reader,

Betsy Ross's Star was a difficult book to write.

In other Blast to the Past books, the kids visit famous American inventors and visionaries. They always know who they are visiting, what the person did, and where they were when they changed the world. Facts, facts, and more facts.

This time the facts were fuzzy. We knew that Betsy Ross's grandson William Canby gave a speech to the Historical Society of Pennsylvania in 1870. In that speech, he said his grandmother made the first American flag, but even William Canby knew there weren't very many facts to back up his claims. And certainly, as Bo kept telling us, there was no hard evidence—no flag designs or receipts existed.

There is also no proof that a congressional committee ever visited Betsy Ross in her shop, asking her to make the flag. In fact there is no proof a committee even existed at all. All we have is a terrific story about George Washington visiting Betsy Ross and a paper five-pointed star found at Sam Wetherill's house in 1925.

Margaret Donaldson Boggs, Betsy Ross's niece in chapter six, wasn't really eleven years old in 1776. She was actually five months old. But she did later sign an affidavit, a letter, saying that Betsy Ross told her she'd made the first "star-spangled banner."

Regarding the five-pointed star in Sam Wetherill's locker: One source we read said the star was found in 1925, while another said 1922. And yet a third reported that it wasn't known about until 1964! According to a man named John Harker, who wrote a book about the star, there is writing on the back that reads "H. C. Wilson/Betsey Ross/Pattern for/ Stars." Apparently Betsy's name is misspelled. Hmmm. You can see the paper star on display at the Free Quaker Meeting House in Philadelphia.

Does all this convince you that Betsy Ross made the first American flag?

We mention Francis Hopkinson in the book because there is a little evidence that he designed the first flag. Four years after Betsy Ross was supposed to have made the flag, Francis Hopkinson sent a receipt to the Continental Congress asking them to pay him for a few things he'd been working on, including the design of the flag. Congress rejected his bill and never paid him. They claimed that he was not the only person who submitted a flag design. Interesting, but it doesn't help us know for certain who made that first flag.

It's also interesting to note that Francis Hopkinson did eventually use five-pointed stars in his flag designs, but not in the one he made for the Continental Congress.

So we are back to Betsy Ross. Did she create that first American flag or not? We might never know. The question we need to ask now is, does it matter?

Thanks for coming on our adventure with us. It's been a blast.

If you want to learn more about the series or want to contact us, you can visit our website at www.BlasttothePastBooks.com.

Stacia and Rhody

Nancy Drew and the Clue Crew®

Test your detective skills with more Clue Crew cases!

Visit NancyDrew.com for the inside scoop!

From Aladdin · KIDS.SimonandSchuster.com

Join Zeus and his friends as they set off on the adventure of a lifetime.

Now Available:

HEROES IN TRAINING

Cronus and the Threads of Dread

Joan Holub &
Suzanne Williams

#1 Zeus and the Thunderbolt of Doom
#2 Poseidon and the Sea of Fury
#3 Hades and the Helm of Darkness
#4 Hyperion and the Great Balls of Fire
#5 Typhon and the Winds of Destruction
#6 Apollo and the Battle of the Birds
#7 Ares and the Spear of Fear